THE PUPPY PLACE

LIBERTY

THE PUPPY PLACE

Don't miss any of these other stories by Ellen Miles!

THE PUPPY PLACE

LIBERTY

ELLEN
MILES

SCHOLASTIC INC.

For Faith Rose

ISBN 978-0-545-55420-6

Cover art by Tim O'Brien
Original cover design by Steve Scott

12 11   19/0

Printed in the U.S.A.   40

First printing, May 2014

CHAPTER ONE

"When will they start?" Lizzie Peterson leaned into her mother's warm hug. She hated to admit it, but she was so sleepy she could hardly keep her eyes open. Still, there was no way she was going to miss the fireworks. She'd been looking forward to them ever since she'd learned that her family was going to Brisco Beach for the Fourth of July.

Lizzie had been hearing about Brisco Beach for years. Her cousins Stephanie and Becky went there every summer. It was a tiny town, mostly made up of vacation cottages, way out on a long, narrow spit of land between the ocean and the bay. Stephanie loved to talk about Brisco Beach.

Lizzie had heard about the bay side (shallow, no waves, great for swimming or paddling in a kayak) and the ocean side (big waves for bodysurfing, great beach for building sandcastles at low tide).

She'd heard about the cottages (adorable, and each with its own cute name), the Snack Shack (best fries anywhere!), Captain Stark's fishing pier (a long, rickety boardwalk that extended far into the ocean, held high above the surf on tall wooden pilings), and The Point (groovy surf shop, best place to buy a bathing suit or ankle bracelet).

Stephanie had told Lizzie how you could ride a bike to any of those places, or walk on the beach for miles, collecting seashells, or, on a rainy afternoon, just lie on the screened-in porch at the cottage and read.

Lizzie thought it sounded like heaven — even without the fireworks. But the fireworks, according to Stephanie, were the very best part. "They don't start until it's dark," she'd told Lizzie that afternoon. "Everybody goes over to the ocean side to wait for them, and there are bonfires all up and down the beach. People play guitars and sing, or have clambakes. We always have hot dogs for dinner and s'mores for dessert. You eat until you can't eat any more, and then the sun goes down and you know the fireworks will happen soon. It gets darker and darker and you wait and wait and wait. It always seems like forever. And then — *BOOM!* — the first one goes off."

Her eyes shone when she talked about that part. "And then they go on, and on, and on. It's the best fireworks show *ever*. At the end, after the big finale, everybody cheers and claps and yells." Her voice sounded dreamy. "It's the best. That's all. Just the best. You'll see."

But would she? Lizzie was starting to wonder. Here she was, at Brisco Beach with her cousins.

The Petersons had rented an extra-large cottage, the Sea 'n' Stars, so everyone could fit into one house. So far Lizzie had discovered that everything Stephanie had told her was true. The Snack Shack fries were the best. The Point was the coolest store ever. Lizzie and Stephanie had hung fishing poles off Captain Stark's pier, and swum on the bay side, and made a whole sandcastle village on the ocean side.

Sometimes Stephanie could be stuck-up about being a year older than Lizzie, but on this vacation they were having a great time together. They'd even begun calling themselves "fruzzins": friends plus cousins.

That night both families had carried a huge picnic down to the beach. They'd made a bonfire and had eaten hot dogs and potato salad and s'mores until Lizzie thought her belly would bust.

But would she ever see the fireworks? Would they ever start?

Now they were all spread out on a patchwork of blankets and beach towels laid over the cooling sand. Becky was curled up on her dad's lap, and Stephanie sat talking quietly to her mom, Lizzie's aunt Abigail. Stephanie flashed a smile at Lizzie through the growing darkness. "Be patient," she called softly. "Stay awake!"

Lizzie smiled back and gave Stephanie a thumbs-up. Then she yawned and looked over at her younger brother Charles, who lay conked out across their dad's legs. Next to them on a red fleece blanket lay her youngest brother, the Bean, already in his pajamas and sleeping soundly. Lizzie knew both boys might sleep through the fireworks — if they ever started — but she was determined not to do that. She had to stay awake.

She opened her eyes wide and stared at the star-spangled sky. It wasn't totally dark out yet; there was still a hint of blue sky near the horizon over the ocean, and a band of pink clouds behind the dunes, where the sun had set.

Boom!

Lizzie sat up straight. "Are they starting?" She didn't see any bright flashes overhead.

Stephanie waved a hand. "Nah, that's another town, way up the beach. Arndale. They always get an earlier start. But their fireworks aren't nearly as good as ours."

Lizzie sighed and lay back against her mother. "What do you think Buddy is doing right now?" she asked. Buddy was the Petersons' brown-and-white puppy, the cutest and best puppy ever.

Buddy had started out as a foster puppy. The Petersons took care of puppies who needed homes, just until they found each one the perfect forever family. But unlike the other puppies, Buddy had come to stay. Now he was at Aunt Amanda's for the week, having his own vacation. Lizzie's aunt Amanda owned a doggy day-care center called Bowser's Backyard, and in the summer she also ran a place called Camp Bowser, a sleepaway camp for dogs.

Lizzie had begged her parents to bring Buddy along to Brisco Beach. "The cottage is pet-friendly," she'd pointed out after she'd seen the brochure that described it. But Mom had said it was complicated enough packing up everything for a family of five, and Charles and Dad had agreed that Buddy would be happier staying with Aunt Amanda. Even Lizzie had to admit that her puppy was probably having the time of his life. Nobody took better care of dogs than Aunt Amanda.

"What's Buddy doing right now? Well, let's see." Mom pulled Lizzie closer. There was a cool salty breeze coming off the ocean, and Mom's fleece jacket felt soft and warm against Lizzie's cheek. "I'll bet Buddy had a fun day chasing butterflies and wading in the stream at Camp Bowser. Your aunt probably gave him some special treat after dinner — maybe some liver brownies or a home-made peanut butter dog biscuit. And now I can just imagine him snoozing away on one of her super-cozy dog beds. Lucky old Buddy."

Lizzie could picture it, too. It gave her a pang to think of Buddy being happy without her, but she knew he was safe and sound with Aunt Amanda. And soon enough she'd be back home with him, and they could snuggle and play and —

BOOM!

A huge umbrella of sparkling red opened wide, high above their heads. Glittering red sparkles rained down toward the dark ocean, trailing red streaks against the starlit sky.

BOOM! BOOM! BOOM!

Green, blue, red. Fountains and bursts and giant flower shapes filled the sky with brilliant colors. Lizzie gasped and pointed, smiling up at the sight. She felt a lump in her throat; something about fireworks always made her feel a little like crying. Maybe it was because they were just so beautiful, so unlike anything else.

"Ooh!" everyone said. "Aaah!"

And then, suddenly, everybody was saying something else. Shouting it, in fact.

"Loose dog!"

"Get him!"

"Catch it!"

As the fireworks boomed above, the people on the beach shouted and yelled and ran, chasing a speedy blur past the bonfires, past the picnics, past the beach chairs and blankets and umbrellas.

Then, out of the twilight, a small furry bundle charged straight toward Lizzie.

It was a puppy.

CHAPTER TWO

Lizzie scrambled to her feet and tried to shake the sleepiness out of her head. The puppy came closer, zigzagging up the beach as it dodged the people who chased it. The puppy's ears were back and its tail was tucked between its legs. Lizzie understood doggy body language. She could see right away that this dog was not out for a fun run. This dog was very, very frightened.

Every muscle in Lizzie's body longed to dive for that running puppy, but she held back. What if she didn't catch it? She would only scare it even more.

Just as she was thinking that, a man in a yellow sweater dove for the puppy and grabbed its collar. "Got it," he yelled.

But the puppy wriggled and pulled and dug its feet into the sand. It backed up, squeezed out of its collar, and took off running once again. "Hey!" The man stood there with the empty collar dangling from his hand. "Get back here."

The puppy didn't even pause. It just kept running, tail between its legs.

Lizzie thought fast. What did she usually do when Buddy ran away from her? "Here, puppy," she called in a high, happy voice. "This way. Let's go!" She began to run — not *toward* the puppy, but away from it, and away from the dark surf. If she could tempt the puppy toward her, the high dunes lining the beach would create a wall that would hem it in. Fireworks burst overhead as she ran across the sand, looking back over her shoulder and calling in that happy voice. "C'mon," she cried as she ran.

The puppy veered toward her. It was working! She ran a few more steps, then let herself tumble to the ground. When she did that with Buddy, he would usually come straight over and joyfully jump on top of her for some hugs and kisses.

But just then there was another huge boom overhead and a shower of gold and silver sparks. A woman behind the puppy tried to grab it. And a man yelled, "That's it! You got it."

The puppy ducked and turned and dashed back the way it had come, straight toward Lizzie's family. Her parents, brothers, aunt and uncle, and cousins had all jumped to their feet.

"Everybody grab some hot dogs," Lizzie yelled. She knew there'd been plenty of leftovers after they had all eaten their fill. "Make a line, and try not to let the puppy through!"

She wasn't sure if she could be heard over the booming overhead, but then she saw her dad dash for the platter of leftover food. Quickly, he passed out pieces of hot dog to everyone standing nearby, and they all spread out in a line across the beach. Strangers joined the line, and soon they blocked the puppy's escape.

The puppy veered away, but Lizzie ran diagonally to get ahead of it again. "Good puppy," she called in that high, happy voice. "Let's go. This way, sweetie!" She ran toward the line of people. If she could just get the puppy close enough to smell those delectable hot dogs . . .

Stephanie waved her hot dog at the puppy. "Here, puppy," she cried in the same happy voice Lizzie was using. She had caught on quickly. "See what I have?"

The puppy slowed down as it came closer to the line of people. Crouching, it looked out toward the surf and up toward the dunes, as if trying to figure out an escape. Stephanie called again. "Yum, yum." She held out the hot dog. "Who wants a treat?"

An older kid Lizzie didn't know was standing next to Stephanie. "Oh, boy," he said loudly. "Hot dogs. I love hot dogs!" He pretended to eat a bite of his. "Want some?" He held it out toward the puppy. The puppy inched closer, sticking its neck out to sniff at the food in the boy's hand.

BOOM! A fountain of green overflowed above their heads. The puppy flinched but did not run. Instead, it stretched its neck out even farther toward the food. "Good dog," said the boy. "Good dog."

By then, except for the fireworks, the beach was quieter. Everybody had stopped shouting and chasing the dog. Lizzie held her breath, hoping everyone understood that the only way to catch the dog was to stop chasing it.

Lizzie pulled her braided rope belt out of the belt loops of her shorts. It wasn't very long, but at least it was something. Without any kind of leash, it would be hard to hang on to the puppy if they did catch it. She made a loop with it and stepped forward quietly, watching as the dog began to nibble at the treat in the boy's hand.

"Good dog," he kept saying. "That's a good dog."

Stephanie handed her piece of hot dog to him, and he held it out to the puppy. "Here's some more," he said as he let the pup chew at it. "Good dog."

The puppy was gobbling so fast that it hardly noticed as Lizzie stepped up behind it and slipped the looped belt over its head.

"Yes," whispered the boy as he handed over the last piece of hot dog. He, Lizzie, and Stephanie all grinned at each other. "Nice work," he said, nodding at Lizzie.

BOOM! BOOMBOOMBOOMBOOM!

The fireworks exploded above them, and the sky was full of color. Red, blue, green, silver, gold — like a cascade of stars, the sparks trailed and twinkled, reflected in the dark surf. Lizzie knelt to hug the trembling puppy close. "It's okay," she said. "We'll keep you safe."

After one last, long burst of *BOOM*s, the fireworks were over. Everyone clapped and whistled and hollered while Lizzie held the puppy tight. Then silence fell on the beach. Now it was truly dark, and the only light came from the twinkle of stars above and the few flickering bonfires still burning along the beach. Lizzie could hear the sound of the surf against the shore.

She felt the warm little body trembling in her arms, and her heart melted. Poor, scared little thing. Where were its people? Lizzie glanced over the puppy's head, sweeping her gaze up and down the beach. Any minute now, somebody would arrive to claim the dog. They'd be out of breath from running, but Lizzie knew how happy they would be to see their beautiful puppy again.

She carried the puppy back to her family's spot and sat down on a plaid blanket to wait. The puppy felt heavy in her arms. After all that running and excitement, it had done what puppies do. It had fallen fast asleep.

CHAPTER THREE

Uncle Stephen and Stephanie walked up the beach, hoping to find the puppy's people. The guy who had helped catch the puppy walked with them, saying he lived in that direction. Mom and Aunt Abigail took Charles, Becky, and the Bean back to the cottage to put them to bed. Dad went off to find more driftwood for the bonfire. And Lizzie sat with the puppy in her arms and waited.

And waited. The beach was totally quiet now except for the "hush, hush" of the incoming tide lapping against the shore. No strangers appeared out of the dark, running after their puppy. No voices called a name over and over, searching for a lost dog. No eager hands reached for a beloved pet. Lizzie knew her dad was close by, but she felt like she and the puppy were all alone in the world.

Now, in the light of the dancing flames, she could get a better look at the puppy. It was a girl, with a long nose, floppy ears, and a long, feathery tail. Her silky fur, the color of a copper penny, shone in the firelight. "You're a little golden retriever girl, aren't you?" Lizzie murmured into the sleeping puppy's ear. "You've got that pretty red color, like Rufus." Rufus was an older golden retriever who lived next door with Charles's best friend, Sammy, back home.

Lizzie was crazy about dogs. She loved to play with them, read about them, and train them. She volunteered at Caring Paws, the local animal shelter; she helped Aunt Amanda at Bowser's Backyard; and she even had a dog-walking business. She had never met a puppy or dog she didn't love. But golden retriever was definitely one of her favorite breeds. In fact, the very first puppy the Petersons had fostered was a golden retriever, a sweet baby girl named Goldie. She'd been only about ten roly-poly weeks old when she arrived at the Petersons'. This new puppy was quite a bit taller and skinnier, with longer legs. She looked older, maybe around four or five months, Lizzie thought.

"I wonder what your name is." Lizzie stroked the puppy's silky ears. The trembling had stopped by now, and the dog was snoring softly. Lizzie could imagine how exhausted she must be after all that running.

Dad came back and put a few pieces of wood on the bonfire, just enough to get it crackling. Then he brought over a blanket and tucked it around Lizzie's shoulders. "We should probably head back to the cottage in a little while, once that fire burns down again," he said. "It's getting late."

"But what about the puppy?" Lizzie asked. "What if her owners come looking for her? I'd be going crazy if Buddy had run off into the dark." Of course, Lizzie knew better than to take Buddy to see a fireworks show. He was a brave little puppy, but loud noises like that would scare just about any dog.

Dad sat down next to her and petted the puppy's head. "We can wait a while longer," he said. "Let's see if your uncle and cousin find anyone. But if not, I think we'll just have to take her with us."

Lizzie smiled into the dark. Dad felt just like she did. Neither of them would ever give up on a puppy who needed their help. They sat quietly together, listening to the sound of the surf. Lizzie leaned against her father and looked up at the stars. There were a zillion of them out here at the beach. She could even see the wide bright swath of the Milky Way. She tried to watch for a falling star, but her eyelids kept drooping. Now that all the excitement was over, she was sleepy again. The puppy was warm and heavy in her arms, and she could feel her dad's chest rise and fall with his breath.

Then Uncle Stephen and Stephanie appeared out of the dark.

Lizzie sat up. The puppy snorted and stuck out a paw, then settled back to sleep. "Did you find anybody?" Lizzie could see that her cousin and uncle were alone, but she still had to ask.

Stephanie shook her head as she plopped down next to Lizzie. "Nope. But we got this back, at least." She held up a red collar. "We ran into the guy who was holding her when she slipped out of it. There's a tag on it, too. Guess what her name is?"

Lizzie shrugged. "How should I know?"

"It's a perfect name for today," Stephanie said. "Come on, fruzzin. Guess!"

Lizzie rolled her eyes. "Fireworks?" she said. "Fourth of July?" Impatiently, she grabbed for the collar dangling from Stephanie's hand. She peered at the silver heart-shaped tag that hung from it. "Liberty!"

The puppy snorted again and rolled over to paw at the collar.

That's my name, all right.

24

"And there's a phone number, too," said Stephanie. "We can call as soon as we get back to the cottage."

Lizzie felt her heart sink. She pulled the puppy tighter to her chest and buried her face in Liberty's sweet-smelling fur. She knew she should be happy that this darling pup would soon be back with her owners. But did it have to happen so soon? As much fun as this vacation had been, it would be even better with a puppy to take care of and play with.

Lizzie had always felt that no matter what you were doing, everything was always more special with a puppy. She had already pictured Liberty jumping into the middle of a sandcastle, or chasing a seagull down the beach. She'd imagined how sweet it would be to have a puppy sleeping at the end of her bed, in the tiny bedroom she shared with Stephanie. But Lizzie knew it was selfish to keep the puppy one second longer than they needed to. Liberty's family must be frantic with worry by now.

She bent to kiss the puppy's neck, just behind the ears, where a puppy's fur is always softest. Then she turned to Stephanie and nodded. "We'll call as soon as we get back," she agreed.

CHAPTER FOUR

While Dad and Uncle Stephen and Stephanie shook the sand off the blankets and made sure the fire was out, Lizzie unbuckled the collar and put it back around the puppy's neck. She threaded her rope belt through the ring where you would usually clip on a leash. "All set," she said. "Ready, Liberty?"

The pup rolled off Lizzie's lap, stretched both front legs way out, and yawned noisily. She shook herself off, wriggling from head to toe, then gazed up at Lizzie with a wary look in her eyes. Her tail was still tucked between her legs.

Um, okay, I guess. Where are we going?

Lizzie sighed. The poor thing was still scared. "It's all right, sweetie. We'll take good care of you. Don't worry." They walked up toward the dunes, shining their flashlights to find the tiny path that led through the tall grasses and over the hill to their neighborhood. Liberty stuck close to Lizzie's side, as if she was afraid of the dark that surrounded them.

Back at the cottage, Mom and Aunt Abigail sat in the kitchen, talking softly and sipping mugs of tea. Mom raised her eyebrows when she saw what Lizzie had at the end of the leash. "You brought the puppy?"

Dad stepped in quickly. "We sort of had to. Nobody showed up to claim her."

"But we found her collar, and it has her name on it and a phone number," Stephanie added. "We can call right now."

Mom glanced at the clock. "It's awfully late to call anyone."

"How could her owners be sleeping?" Lizzie asked. "I'd never go to sleep if Buddy was missing. I would stay up all night looking for him."

"Good point," said Mom.

"What's her name, anyway?" Aunt Abigail got up from her chair and came over to kneel by the puppy. "What's your name, you little sweetheart? What a cutie you are." Liberty snuggled up to Aunt Abigail and put a paw on her knee.

"Her name's Liberty," said Lizzie.

"Isn't that perfect?" Stephanie asked. "For a dog we found on the Fourth of July?" She knelt down, too. "Liberty," she crooned. "Sweet Liberty."

Lizzie looked at her dad and raised her eyebrows. He smiled back. They both knew that Stephanie and Becky had been wishing for a dog. It was a good sign that Aunt Abigail liked Liberty. Maybe, if they didn't find her owners . . .

Lizzie shook her head. She was getting ahead of herself. Nobody was going to adopt this puppy — not until she had done everything she could to find Liberty's real owners. "I guess we should call," she said.

Dad nodded and reached for the phone. "What's the number?" he asked.

Lizzie looked at the tag on Liberty's collar and read the number while Dad dialed. Then she kissed Liberty on the nose. "Good girl," she said. "Soon we'll know where you belong."

Dad spoke into the phone. "Hello, my name is Paul Peterson. I'm calling about your dog, Liberty. We found her on the beach. You can reach us at —" He put his hand over the phone. "What's the number here?"

Lizzie's mother grabbed the cottage's information sheet from the counter and handed it to Dad.

"We're at Sea 'n' Stars, in Brisco. Call anytime. We'll take good care of Liberty until we hear from you." He hung up. "Voice mail," he said. "They're probably still out looking for her."

"Tomorrow we can check with the police in town," said Aunt Abigail.

"And maybe we should put up some signs, too." Lizzie yawned and stretched. "I'll make them in the morning. Want to help, Steph?"

"Um, sure," said Stephanie. She was still petting Liberty.

"And then we can go around on our bikes and put them up. And after that we can take Liberty to the beach and make another sandcastle village. And —"

"And none of that's going to happen unless you two get some sleep first," Mom said firmly. "Let's get that puppy outside to do her business one last time, and then you girls need to head off to bed."

"But what if Liberty's owners call?" Lizzie asked.

"I'll answer the phone if it rings," Dad promised. "They can pick her up first thing in the morning."

Lizzie and Stephanie took Liberty outside and walked her around the block. The little neighborhood of cottages was cozy and sweet. Yellow light beamed from a few windows here and there, but most cottages were dark. Lizzie pictured everyone sleeping soundly, tucked in their beds, probably dreaming of fireworks. She was definitely ready to be tucked in herself.

Lizzie yawned. "Well, at least Liberty gets to sleep in our room tonight."

"On my bed," Stephanie said.

"No way." Lizzie stopped to face her, hands on hips.

"Just kidding, fruzzin," Stephanie said. "She can be on your bed half the time, too." She grinned. "At least we don't also have to share her with Charles and the Bean and Becky, since they're already asleep."

Lizzie glanced down at the pretty pup who walked between them, sniffing the salty sea air. Lizzie felt a pang in her stomach as she reached down to stroke Liberty's soft head. "And they might never even meet her. By the time we all wake up, she might be gone."

The funny thing was, when Lizzie woke up the next morning, it wasn't Liberty who was gone.

CHAPTER FIVE

Lizzie first woke just as the dawn's light peeked through the little round porthole window next to her bed, but her sleeping bag felt cozy, and Liberty was snuggled up next to her. "Yay," she whispered softly to the pup, who lay with her muzzle across Lizzie's shoulder. "You're still here."

She knew she should get Liberty outside for a pee, but since the puppy seemed content to sleep a little longer, Lizzie decided she was, too. Anyway, Stephanie was still snoring softly in her bed. Lizzie squirmed deeper down inside her sleeping bag, hugged Liberty closer, and dozed off.

When she woke again an hour later, the sun was shining brightly. Liberty was licking her face and making little whining noises.

Time to get up. Let's get going! We have to find my people, remember?

Lizzie unzipped her sleeping bag and sat up. "Hey, fruzzin, wake up. Looks like someone's ready to start the day," she called to her cousin as she stretched and yawned. But when she looked over at Stephanie's bed, it was empty. That was strange. Stephanie usually slept as late as she could.

Lizzie pulled on her Brisco Beach uniform: bathing suit and shorts. She stepped into her flip-flops and headed downstairs with Liberty trotting close behind her. Mom and Aunt Abigail were bustling around in the kitchen, and the warm, sunny room smelled sweet and delicious.

"Where's Stephanie?" Lizzie asked. "Did Liberty's people call? What smells so good?"

Mom laughed. "Out on her bike, not yet, and your aunt's famous French toast, in that order. But before you have any, you'd better get that puppy out for a pee."

Lizzie pushed open the sliding doors and stepped out onto the deck. The sun was shining brightly in a blue, blue sky and there was a soft, ocean-smelling breeze. Seagulls circled and screeched overhead. "Come on, Liberty," she said as she headed down the wooden stairs to the backyard. "It's a beautiful day." The puppy padded cautiously down the stairs beside her.

Are we going to see my people now? I really do miss them.

By the time Lizzie and Liberty got back from their walk, the kitchen was full of people. Becky and Charles sat at the table, eating French toast drenched in syrup, and the Bean sat on Dad's lap. "Uppy!" the Bean shouted when he saw Liberty. He struggled to get down.

Liberty hung back, behind Lizzie's knees. "It's okay," Lizzie told the pup. "Everybody here is a friend."

Charles and Becky jumped up to pet the pup.

"Easy," said Lizzie. "She's a little timid. Go slow."

"She's so cute." Charles held out a hand for Liberty to sniff. "Who could guess that we would find a foster puppy at the beach?"

Lizzie saw Aunt Abigail and Mom exchange glances. "Let's not get ahead of ourselves," said Mom. "We'll probably hear from her owners very soon."

"I can't believe they haven't called yet." Lizzie

set out a bowl of water for the puppy. "We'll have to buy Liberty some food. She must be starving by now."

"I'll head out right after breakfast," Mom promised. "I have a few other things to pick up at the store. And I'll check in at the local police station, too. Maybe they've heard something about a missing dog."

"I'll come with you," said Lizzie. "We can bring Liberty, and they can scan her to see if she has a microchip." She sat down at the table and Aunt Abigail handed her a plate piled with thick, delicious-smelling French toast. Lizzie ate quickly, feeling guilty whenever she looked down at Liberty's pleading face. "We can pick up some paper and markers, too, so we can make some Lost Dog signs."

"I'll help," said Charles.

"Me, too," said Becky.

"Me, three!" said the Bean. He proudly held up three fingers.

Everybody cracked up — except for Lizzie. She looked at the spot where Stephanie usually sat at meals. Why wasn't she around to help? "Where did Stephanie *go*, anyway?"

"I'm not sure," said Aunt Abigail. "She and her dad both headed out before I was up." Aunt Abigail did not seem worried.

Lizzie finished her breakfast and brought her plate to the sink. Becky and Charles chattered about how cute Liberty was and all the things they wanted to do with her that day, but Lizzie was lost in thought. Why hadn't her fruzzin waited for her to wake up? Didn't she want to help with Liberty? Sometimes Stephanie was a real mystery.

"Don't forget, Stephanie's a little older than you," her mom said as they drove to the store.

"She might just need some time on her own now and then."

Lizzie petted Liberty, stroking her silky ears. She knew Mom was right, but her feelings were still hurt. She tried to let it go. She had more important things to think about — like the adorable puppy curled up on her lap. "What if Liberty's owners don't call?" she asked.

"We'll cross that bridge when we come to it," said Mom.

"Bridge?" Lizzie asked. "What bridge? Where?"

"It's a saying," Mom said as she pulled up next to a low white building. A small sign said TOWN OFFICES, BRISCO BEACH. "I guess this is where we'd find the police."

But when they went up to the door, there was a hand-lettered sign on it that said CLOSED FOR THE HOLIDAY. IF AN EMERGENCY, PLEASE CALL STATE POLICE.

"It's not exactly an emergency." Lizzie looked down at the puppy by her side. "After all, Liberty is safe and sound with us, and we've called her owners."

"I suppose you're right," said Mom. "It looks as if we're stuck with this puppy for a little longer." She sounded grumpy, but Lizzie could see that she was smiling as she bent to ruffle Liberty's ears.

CHAPTER SIX

Back at the cottage, Stephanie walked into the kitchen just as Lizzie was setting out the supplies she'd bought for making signs. "Where were you?" Lizzie asked.

Stephanie shrugged. "Just out, riding around." She pulled a chair up to the kitchen table. "What are you doing?"

Lizzie didn't answer right away. She wondered if Stephanie was even still her fruzzin. She pulled a few more markers out of the bag. "Making posters," she said finally as she arranged them next to a stack of paper. "About

Liberty. We don't have a computer or a copier or anything, so we have to write them all by hand."

Stephanie grabbed a piece of paper and a marker. "I'll help."

Soon Charles and Becky and the Bean joined them, too. Lizzie wrote out what she wanted the posters to say so they could all copy it. At the top it said:

FOUND! LOST DOG

Then, on the bottom, she wrote:

Golden retriever puppy. Name: Liberty.
Found on: Brisco Beach, Fourth of July
Call Sea 'n' Stars, Brisco Beach, if you are
looking for Liberty!

Then, in the middle of each sign, they all drew pictures of Liberty, since they couldn't print out a picture from Lizzie's camera, the way they usually did. Lizzie worked hard on hers. She blended three colors of crayons — red, brown, and burnt orange — until she had just the right shade for Liberty's coat. She drew carefully, putting in lots of detail like Liberty's short, dark whiskers and the pretty feathering on her tail. When she was done, she held it up to admire it.

"Nice," said Stephanie, leaning over to see it. Becky and Charles liked it, too.

"All done," said the Bean. He held up his own picture.

"Wow!" said Lizzie and Stephanie together. Lizzie couldn't believe it. The Bean was only a toddler, but his drawing was better than hers. Sure, it didn't have the detail — but there was something about his loopy scrawling picture, all in bright red crayon. Somehow, he had captured Liberty's spirit perfectly.

"How did you *do* that?" Lizzie asked her little brother.

The Bean just laughed his googly laugh.

"He's going to be an artist someday," Stephanie predicted, bending down to give him a squeeze. "Aren't you, little cuz?"

After lunch, Lizzie and Stephanie decided to walk Liberty downtown to put up posters while Mom and Aunt Abigail drove Charles, Becky, and the Bean "up-island" to hang some more signs in the next two towns.

"Let's go to the Snack Shack first," Lizzie suggested as they headed down the driveway. She liked the owners there, Angelo and Debbie. They were the friendliest people she had ever met. They always had something funny to say, and they'd give you an extra with your order, like free sprinkles on your cone. Debbie even remembered that Lizzie preferred rainbow sprinkles, while Charles liked chocolate. Lizzie grinned at her fruzzin and held up a five-dollar bill. "Mom said we could get small cones for a treat." That was the great thing about vacation: dessert after just about every meal.

"Now, where did that adorable pup come from?" Debbie asked, staring through the Snack Shack's window at Liberty a few minutes later. Liberty wagged her tail tentatively and leaned against Lizzie's leg. "Aww, she's a shy one, isn't she?"

"We found her." Lizzie held up the poster with the Bean's picture. "And now we're trying to find her owners. You're right, she's a little shy, but probably only because she's missing her people."

Debbie took the poster. "Well, isn't that the cutest thing? We'll just slap this up in our window, right next to the Special Sundae of the Day sign.

Everybody who's anybody stops by here at least once a day." She taped the poster up right away. "Now, what can I get you two darlin's? Let me guess. Two small cones, one vanilla with rainbow sprinkles and the other just plain chocolate. Am I right?" A moment later, she handed the cones through the window. "What about the pup? Think she'd like one? Lots of folks bring their dogs here for ice cream. Vanilla only, of course, since chocolate is bad for dogs."

Lizzie looked down at Liberty. The puppy looked back at her with pleading eyes.

That looks so delicious. My people would never let me have something like that. But maybe you will!

Lizzie was tempted. But she knew it probably wasn't a good idea. "Better not," she said. "We don't know if her owners would like that. Maybe she has a sensitive tummy."

"Thanks anyway." Stephanie tugged on Lizzie's arm. "Come on. We have a lot more posters to put up."

They strolled along, licking their cones and stopping to tape up posters on light poles and bulletin boards. They went to the Red and White supermarket, the Brisco Beach Historical Society and Weather Station, and the Happy Pelican seafood store. Finally, they came to the last shop in the row, the one nearest to the beach. The Point.

"Think they'll mind if we bring Liberty in?" Lizzie asked. She'd seen dogs in there before. It was a pretty casual kind of store.

"I'll go check," said Stephanie. She smoothed her hair and pushed open the door. A moment later she was back. "Bring her on in," she said.

Liberty was a hit at The Point. The owner, a tattooed guy named Bear, made a big fuss over her. Even though Bear was a big, muscle-y guy, he seemed to understand how to pet the puppy gently so she wouldn't be scared of him. "Hey," Lizzie said to Stephanie as they pinned their sign to the bulletin board. She pointed to the photo of a guy in a "Meet The Point Employees" photo collage. His floppy blond hair and bright blue eyes looked familiar. "Isn't that the guy who helped us catch Liberty?"

Stephanie peered at the picture. She shrugged. "Maybe. Who knows? It was dark. Hey, let's take Liberty to the beach. We can put up a poster at the fishing pier."

Lizzie smiled. Maybe Stephanie still wanted to be fruzzins after all. They scrambled over the dunes in back of The Point and spent the rest of the afternoon collecting shells, wading in the surf,

49

...d building a tall sandcastle just for Liberty to jump on and destroy.

Dinner that night was fried clams from the Snack Shack. Afterward, everyone sat out on the deck to watch the sun go down and the stars come out.

Even though the day had gone by with no sign of Liberty's owners, Lizzie drifted happily off to sleep that night. When she woke up the next morning with Liberty curled up next to her, she smiled. This vacation was turning out to be the best one ever.

But when she rolled over to say so to Stephanie . . . her fruzzin's bed was empty again.

CHAPTER SEVEN

That Stephanie. Lizzie decided not to let it bother her. So what if her so-called fruzzin wanted to go off by herself? Lizzie could have fun on her own, too. Especially because she wouldn't *be* on her own. She'd be with Liberty. "Right?" she asked the red pup. "What do you say? Want to go outside?"

Liberty jumped off the bed and shook herself, wriggling from tail to nose, then stretched waaaay out with her front feet forward and her butt in the air.

Sure, let's go. Maybe today I'll finally find my people.

Lizzie dressed quickly — bathing suit and shorts again — and headed upstairs. This time she didn't even bother asking where Stephanie was. She just grabbed a bagel and found the piece of clothesline they were using for a leash. "Going out for a while," she called to her mom, who was sitting on the deck with Aunt Abigail.

"Don't be too long without letting us know where you are," Mom called back. "Remember, we might get a call any minute about Liberty."

Lizzie was starting to wonder about that. Would Liberty's owners *ever* call? She couldn't understand why they had not answered any of the messages Dad had left. He had been calling every couple of hours, but every time he got their voice mail.

"See you," Lizzie called to Dad and Uncle Stephen as she passed the garage. They were checking out their fishing gear.

"Keep an eye on the weather," Dad said. "I heard on the radio this morning that there might be a storm blowing in."

Lizzie looked up at the sky. She already felt hot and sticky even though the morning sun was having a hard time breaking through a bank of gray clouds. "I hope not," she said. "I want to take Liberty swimming on the bay side later on." She gave a gentle tug on the leash. "Let's go, Liberty." She was thinking she might head downtown first, just to see if she ran into Stephanie. Not that she'd expect to hang out with her. In fact, Lizzie thought, she might just pretend she didn't see Stephanie. She might turn around, go her own way with her head held high. That would show her so-called fruzzin.

She'd gone only a block or so when Liberty stopped in her tracks. The puppy tucked her tail between her legs and stood trembling, her ears

53

pricked up and her head cocked to one side. "What is it?" Lizzie asked. "Come on, sweetie. You're fine. Everything's okay." She tugged on the leash, but Liberty would not move. Instead, she dug in her heels and started to whimper.

"Liberty?" Lizzie asked. "What's the matter?" She turned all around, trying to figure out what might be bothering the puppy, but the street was empty. No scary people. Nobody on a bike. No other dogs. Not even a squirrel.

Now Liberty began to pull on the leash, trying to drag Lizzie back to the house. "Where are we going?" Lizzie asked. "What has gotten into you?"

Then she heard it. A long, low rumble, far off in the distance.

Thunder.

Before Lizzie even had a moment to think, Liberty jumped straight up in the air, yanking the rope out of Lizzie's hands. Then she took off running, dragging the rope behind her. "Liberty, wait!" Lizzie yelled, but it was no use. That puppy could run.

Liberty zigged and zagged, running wildly down the street. Lizzie dashed after her, hoping that Liberty would head straight back to the cottage so she could yell to Dad and Uncle Stephen to grab the dog. But the puppy seemed to be panicking. Liberty ran straight past the house, galloping one way, then another. She dove into some bushes and popped out again, running the opposite way.

"Dad, help! Liberty's loose!" Lizzie yelled as loudly as she could as she dashed past the garage. Dad popped his head out just in time to see the disappearing dog. He dropped his fishing pole and joined Lizzie. They ran after Liberty, calling her name over and over.

"I think she's headed downtown now," Lizzie said. "Maybe she's following the same route we took yesterday." She and Dad trotted along, catching an occasional glimpse of Liberty cowering for a moment behind a house or dashing across someone's lawn.

By the time they reached the Snack Shack, Lizzie was out of breath. She was frustrated, too, and angry with herself. How could she have let Liberty get away? The poor puppy was probably scared to death. "Have you seen Liberty?" Lizzie panted when Debbie slid the snack bar's window open.

"You mean that pretty pup you had with you yesterday?" Debbie asked. "Oh, dear. No, I can't say that I have. Hey, Angelo," she yelled toward the back. "Seen a puppy?"

After a moment, she shook her head. "Sorry," Debbie said. "Keep us posted. And we'll keep an eye out."

"Maybe she went to The Point," Lizzie said to her dad. "Bear was really nice to her yesterday."

Dad didn't ask who Bear was. He just followed Lizzie as she ran, checking down every alleyway and cross street. She hadn't seen even so much as a flash of red fur for a while now. Where was Liberty? Another rumble of thunder sounded overhead, closer this time.

Lizzie pushed the door open to The Point. Bear was in back, working on a surfboard. "Have you seen that puppy?" she asked before she'd even stopped moving. Dad was right behind her.

Bear looked up. "Puppy?" He shook his head. "No puppy in here."

A boy stepped out from behind a rack of bathing suits. Lizzie recognized him right away. It was the guy from the night of the fireworks, the one who'd helped catch Liberty.

"She ran away again?" he asked.

Lizzie nodded.

"I'll help find her," he said. "Where's Stephanie?"

Lizzie stared at him. How did he know her cousin's name? Then she remembered. That night, this guy had headed up the beach with Stephanie and Uncle Stephen. "I don't know. She left before I got up this morning."

Now the boy stared back at Lizzie. "Oh, no," he said. "She must be down by the pier, looking for me. And that storm is blowing in fast."

As if to underline his words, a clap of thunder boomed, right overhead. Lizzie felt the floor shake beneath her feet.

"We have to find both of them — now!" said the boy.

Dad stepped forward. "Of course we do. But first, would you mind telling me who you are?"

CHAPTER EIGHT

"Dad!" Lizzie was embarrassed. Plus, she couldn't stand to wait for one more second. She had to find Liberty, and Stephanie. Her fruzzin needed her.

But the guy didn't seem to mind. "I'm Ben." He stepped forward and held out his hand for a shake. "I met Stephanie and her dad the night of the fireworks, when we caught Liberty. Then they both came down to the pier early yesterday morning, to watch me and some other people surf."

Lizzie stared at him. So that was where Stephanie had been. Why couldn't she just have said so? Now Lizzie remembered that Uncle

Stephen had not been around at breakfast time, either. But the boy was still talking.

"They were going to come back today, too — to meet my best buddy, Luka." He whistled, and a strong, young yellow Lab stood up from his bed in a corner, shook himself off, and ambled toward them. "Luka can help find Liberty. I'm sure of it. He's got a great nose."

As if to illustrate Ben's statement, Luka put his nose to the hem of Lizzie's shorts and began to snuffle. She could tell that he smelled Liberty's scent.

"I never thought anyone would go to the pier today, considering the weather report," said Ben. He clipped a leash onto Luka's collar and headed for the door. "Later, Bear," he called as he led the way out.

Dad and Lizzie looked at each other and shrugged. It seemed as if Ben had a plan. That was more than Lizzie had. She stepped out, following Ben, and felt the slap of rain in her face. "Whoa!" she said as she held the door open against the wind. "That storm sure is coming in fast." The sky had lowered and darkened, and the blowing rain and wind flattened the tall grasses against the dunes.

Ben turned back toward her and cupped an ear. "What?"

Lizzie could barely hear him over the wind. "Never mind." She shook her head. "Which way?" She mouthed the words with a lot of exaggeration and held up her hands in a questioning gesture. Before he could answer, there was a flash of lightning, way off at the horizon. When a roll of thunder boomed a few moments later, Lizzie jumped. This was getting scary. Where were Stephanie and Liberty?

She felt Dad's hand on her shoulder, as if he

was telling her that he was right there with her. That felt good. "The storm is still a few miles away," Dad shouted, right next to her ear. "We have a little time."

Lizzie saw Luka pull Ben into the dunes, straight up the hidden path that she and Stephanie and Liberty had taken less than twenty-four hours earlier. "He probably just smells our trail from yesterday," she yelled to Ben, but her words were snatched away by the wind.

Ben plunged forward, leading them up and over the rolling swells of grass-covered sand.

When they came down on the other side, emerging from the shelter of the high dunes, Lizzie could hardly believe her eyes. She had never seen the ocean looking like *that*. The water was dark and angry and full of crazy movement, spitting white foam from the peak of every choppy wave. The waves collided with each other and with the shore, careening wildly instead of rolling in orderly rows toward the beach, the way they usually did. The heavy gray sky seemed to hang only a few feet over the water, and there wasn't a seagull or a sandpiper to be seen.

Lizzie saw another flash of lightning, a bright jagged trail against the far horizon. She felt a trembling in her legs and thought of Liberty. How terrified the little pup must be. And if she had gotten confused and run toward the water . . . Lizzie could hardly look at the tossing waves without picturing the way they could sweep away a small red dog in no time at all.

"Which way?" she yelled again to Ben, but then she saw that he had already started running down the beach, toward the fishing pier. Luka loped ahead of him, nose to the ground as he strained at the leash.

Dad grabbed Lizzie's hand. "Let's run," he

shouted. Together, they raced down the beach, toward the long, tall wooden pier, which Lizzie could barely see through the blowing rain. Staying close to the dunes gave them shelter from the wind and a little safety from the storm, but the sand was softer there and harder to move through.

Lizzie knew from building sandcastles that the sand would be firmer near the water, but she was not interested in getting any closer to those roiling waves than she had to. She kicked off her flip-flops and stumbled along, digging her feet into the wet sand.

BOOM! Thunder banged overhead. Lizzie ran faster, as fast as she could. Now she could see Captain Stark's pier more clearly. The waves bashed against the tall pilings that marched out into the ocean, and Lizzie wondered how the pier could hold up against them. Stephanie had told her that the pier had fallen into the ocean years earlier, during a hurricane, and the whole thing had to be rebuilt.

"Look!" Ben was jumping up and down, waving and yelling. "There's somebody there." He and Luka sprinted for the pier, and Lizzie dug down deep to find the energy to push herself a little faster. She squinted through the gloom and spotted something — a person? — huddled under the pier.

"Is that Stephanie?" Dad yelled.

"I can't tell," Lizzie yelled back. But then, as she got closer, she could see a splash of coppery red. A dog, cradled in a person's arms. The person stood up and started to dance around and wave her arms frantically while the dog cowered at her feet.

It was Stephanie. Stephanie and Liberty!

CHAPTER NINE

The storm burst forth with a flash and a boom right overhead just as Lizzie, Dad, Ben, and Luka reached Stephanie. She and Liberty were both trembling. Lizzie gave her fruzzin a quick hug, then bent down to comfort Liberty. The pup was panting and shaking hard. Lizzie petted her in long, calming strokes, but the trembling did not stop.

I'm so scared. Where are my people? I need them.

"Let's get out of here," Ben shouted over the crashing waves. "I've got a key to Captain Stark's shack. He lets me keep some stuff in there. It's not much, but it's shelter."

Lizzie could only make out every other word, but she understood that Ben knew of a place where they could get out of the storm. "Come on," she said to Stephanie. She grabbed Liberty's collar and realized that the length of clothesline was still attached. Poor Liberty must have been dragging that rope behind her the whole time. "Let's go, girl."

She pulled lightly on the rope, trying to coax the terrified pup to move. But Liberty pulled back. The whites of her eyes showed as she bucked and tugged. Lizzie could tell that she was scared out of her mind. "Dad," she yelled. "Can you just pick her up? She's not moving."

Dad came over in two quick strides. He gathered Liberty into his arms. She struggled for a moment, then went limp.

"This way." Between claps of thunder, Ben waved them out from under the pier and they ran, slipping and sliding, up the slope of the dunes until they reached the tiny shack that sat at the entrance to the pier. On sunny days, Captain Stark — or at least a guy who might be Captain Stark — sat in the shack, taking two dollars from each person who wanted to walk out onto his pier to fish or take in the view.

Today the door and windows were shut tight against the storm. A big, rusty padlock hung from the door handle. Ben pulled a key out of his pocket. After fumbling a bit, he managed to open the lock. When he pushed the door open, it slammed against the inside wall, battered by the wind.

They all filed into the cabin, cramming themselves into the tiny space. Dad sat down in a corner, cradling Liberty in his arms, and Lizzie sat next to him.

"Whew," said Ben. "That's better."

It was better. Just having four walls around them and a roof over their heads made Lizzie feel a million times safer. She petted Liberty, talking to her in soothing tones. She knew it wasn't good to baby a frightened pup. Sometimes that could only make them into bigger scaredy-dogs, like Moose, a Great Dane her family had fostered.

She kept her voice matter-of-fact. "It's all good," she told the pup. "We're safe now. No problem. Everything's okay." Liberty's trembling eased up, but she was still panting. She buried her nose in the crook of Dad's arm, as if trying to hide under the covers.

As soon as her heartbeat slowed down a bit, Lizzie began to look around. She saw Ben hand Stephanie an old green blanket to wrap herself in. She noticed how Luka watched Ben's every move. Lizzie also saw two surfboards leaning against a corner of the shack, next to some fishing rods, and realized that they must belong to Ben.

Soon the booming thunder wasn't quite as close anymore, and the pounding of rain on the tin roof had turned to a pattering. Lizzie realized that she had not seen a flash of lightning for a few minutes, and that the surf was not roaring as loudly as it had been. She craned her neck to glance out the window behind her and saw a patch of blue sky.

"It's over," she said just as one more crack of thunder boomed, echoing over the vast ocean. "Well, almost."

"I'm not going anywhere until it's *really* over," Stephanie said in a small voice.

"I don't blame you," said Ben. "That was a scary storm. I can't believe you got caught out in it. I'm so sorry. I never thought you'd come to the pier today."

"I wanted to see Luka surf." Stephanie pulled the blanket closer around her.

"Surf? Your dog knows how to surf?" Lizzie stared at Ben, then at Luka, who had leapt to his feet when he heard the word.

Ben laughed. "Not only does he know how, it's just about his favorite thing in the world. He loves being out there, riding the waves."

"I never heard of a dog that could surf," said Dad.

"I have!" Lizzie suddenly remembered a video she'd seen online. "They have whole surfing contests for dogs. And there's this one amazing dog who helps disabled people learn to surf —"

"I've seen that video!" Ben nodded excitedly. "That's the coolest thing ever. That's what I want

Luka to be able to do someday." He nodded at Liberty. "If she could get over some of her fearfulness, I think Liberty could surf, too. We should get her on a surfboard."

Lizzie's ears perked up. Maybe, if Liberty's owners never showed up — maybe Ben wanted another dog. Maybe he would be the perfect new owner for the red pup. She would have to talk to him about that.

Ben stood up to look out the window. "Sweet." He stretched out his arms to the blue sky. "The storm is over. It's totally cleared up. You can even see the Arndale lighthouse again." He reached for one of the surfboards. "And the waves are still high. Perfect for surfing. Ready, Luka?"

"Wait, did you say Arndale?" That sounded familiar to Lizzie. "Arndale. Isn't that a town way up north? The place where they start their fireworks early?"

Ben smiled at her. "That's right," he said. "How did you —"

But Lizzie wasn't listening. "Dad." She grabbed her father's arm. "We have to drive up to Arndale. Now!"

CHAPTER TEN

"Arndale?" Dad asked.

Lizzie jumped up, and Liberty jumped up, too. Now that the storm was over, she had stopped trembling so much. She even wagged her tail a tiny bit and moved toward the door, as if she was ready to go.

I think I'd like to go find my people now, if that's all right.

"That must be where Liberty came from," Lizzie said. "I never thought of it before, but now it all makes sense."

Stephanie was nodding. "Right," she said. "Because their fireworks go off first."

"I don't get it," said Ben.

"Liberty ran much farther, and much faster, than we ever could have guessed." Lizzie was almost too excited to talk. "She must have started running the minute those other fireworks started, way up in Arndale. The reason her family hasn't seen our signs is that we only put them up around here. Even when Mom drove up north, she didn't go nearly far enough."

"That makes sense. But it doesn't explain why her owners haven't returned my phone calls," said Dad.

"No, but there must be a reason for that, too." Lizzie tugged on her dad's sleeve. "Can we go? Now?"

Before Dad could answer, there was a loud knocking at the door. When Ben pulled it open,

Uncle Stephen was standing there. "Oh, thank goodness," he said when he saw Stephanie. "We were so worried about you. I wondered if you had come down here again."

"Ben found me," Stephanie said. "Well, first Liberty found me. Then the others came along. We got into this place just in time."

Lizzie saw the way Stephanie was looking at Ben, and suddenly she understood everything. Stephanie had a crush on Ben! That was why she had tried to keep him a secret. Lizzie rolled her eyes. Stephanie probably didn't want to be seen with Lizzie because she didn't want Ben to think of her as a little kid. Whatever. Fine.

Lizzie stepped forward. "And guess what? We just figured out that Liberty might be from Arndale," she told her uncle.

Uncle Stephen laughed. "You figured right," he said. "That's another reason I came looking for you.

Your mom went back to the police station this morning. It turns out that the police in Arndale faxed down a sign that Liberty's owners had been posting up there, about their lost dog. They're vacationing here, too. The sign says that the phone number on her tags is no good because it's their home number, and it gave a cell phone number instead. We already called — and they're on their way down right now."

Lizzie stared at him. "Really?" she asked.

"Really. If we call to tell her where we are, I bet your mom will bring Liberty's people here."

She looked down at Liberty. "Did you hear that?" she asked. "Your people are on their way."

Liberty wagged her feathery tail, almost as if she understood.

"Cool," said Ben. "So we're all good. Let's go check out those waves." He picked up his surfboard again and headed for the door, with Luka prancing behind him.

A few moments later, they were all gathered on the beach. "I'll head out on my own first," Ben said, "just to make sure the waves aren't too high for Luka. Can you hold him so he doesn't follow me?" He handed Luka's leash to Stephanie.

Lizzie saw Stephanie blush, and she knew she had been right. Stephanie definitely had a crush on Ben, which was a little ridiculous, because he had to be at least seventeen — way too old for her.

Ben waded into the water, lay down on his board, and paddled out, far into the ocean. The waves looked enormous to Lizzie; even then, after the storm had passed, they were much higher than she'd ever seen them. "He's brave," she said to Stephanie.

"I know." Stephanie didn't take her eyes off Ben.

They all stood and watched as Ben waited for the right wave, paddling to keep himself away from the dangerous pier. Lizzie could see that you had to know what you were doing out there. She turned to Stephanie again. "If a wave smashed you into one of those giant wooden pilings, you'd be —"

"He's up!" said Stephanie, and they all cheered as Ben rode a wave to shore, balancing perfectly and looking cooler than cool.

"Wow," said Lizzie when Ben came ashore. "That's amazing. Can you teach me next summer?"

"Sure," said Ben. "I'll teach everyone." He took Luka's leash from Stephanie. "Ready, pal?" He and Luka waded back into the water. Ben lifted Luka onto the surfboard and the big dog planted all four feet, balancing carefully as Ben pushed the board deeper into the water. This time, Ben did not go out nearly as far. When he turned the board around, Lizzie could swear she saw a smile on the yellow Lab's face. And then — Luka was surfing! Ben gave the board a gentle push at just the right moment, and the dog rode the wave to shore, grinning a doggy grin as he shifted his weight from paw to paw.

Everyone applauded. "That's incredible," said Lizzie's dad. "I've never seen anything like it."

Luka barked happily and charged back into the surf. Ben laughed. "This is the hard part — getting him to stop. He loves it so much." He helped Luka back on the board and towed him out again.

"Hello!" someone called from behind Lizzie.

Liberty leapt to her feet and whirled around to face the dunes. Her ears perked up and she let out three loud, happy barks.

My people! I knew they would find me.

The shiny red pup dashed off, pulling the rope out of Lizzie's hands, and tore up the beach, throwing herself at a group of people who were walking toward them. She leapt up on each of them in turn: a mother, a father, and a teenage girl. Lizzie could hear the people laughing and saying Liberty's name over and over again.

"Well, I guess there's no question about it," Lizzie's dad said to her. "Those are Liberty's people, all right."

As they drew closer, Lizzie could see how happy the people looked. The girl, who was a few years older than Stephanie, was crying a little — but they were obviously tears of relief.

"We can't thank you enough for taking care of Liberty," said the father, shaking Lizzie's hand after they'd all introduced themselves.

"We were worried sick," said the mother. "But we're thrilled to see her again."

The girl didn't say anything. She just plopped down on the beach and let Liberty climb all over her.

Lizzie couldn't believe how confident the red pup seemed now. There was no more trembling. Her feathery tail waved high in the air, her ears were perked up, and she whimpered with joy.

"Somebody sure is happy," said Ben, coming up to join them with a surfboard under his arm and Luka at his side. He was talking about Liberty, but Lizzie could see that he was gazing at the girl the same way Stephanie had gazed at him. "That Liberty is one terrific pup. I'd be happy to teach her how to surf, if you want to bring her down here some morning."

"That would be awesome," said the girl. "Can we start tomorrow?"

Lizzie glanced at Stephanie, who was staring down at the sand. She went over and put her arms around her cousin. "Hey," she whispered. "Now that Liberty's safe, how about if we go celebrate with some Snack Shack fries? Then we can go build a whole sandcastle city. What do you say?"

"I'd say that sounds pretty good," said Stephanie with a tiny smile.

They both gave Liberty one last hug and then they said good-bye and headed off down the beach. Lizzie glanced over her shoulder at the happy group. She was sorry to say good-bye, but she knew Liberty was in good hands. And she still had four more days to enjoy Brisco Beach — with her very best fruzzin.

PUPPY TIPS

The idea for this story first came to me when I was at an outdoor concert last summer. I was talking to the lady sitting next to me, who had a very cute black dog with her. As I petted the dog and asked about its breed (it was a rare French Water Dog, also known as a Barbet), the orchestra was playing. When they got to a certain part in the piece, fireworks began to explode above the stage. The dog jumped up and ran off, trailing its leash behind it! The woman found her dog that night, but the scene stayed with me and I knew it — or something like it — would be a great way to start a Puppy Place book.

I agree with Lizzie: a fireworks show is no place to bring a dog. Many dogs are terrified by loud noises, and losing your dog at night in a big crowd is no fun.

Dear Reader

Guess what? I finally got a puppy! I've been wanting another dog for a long time, ever since my old dog Django died. It took a while to find just the right puppy, but now I have. Zipper is a hound mix with big feet, long legs, and the cutest droopy ears. I love him so much! He is sweet and funny and loving, and he lives up to his name every day as he zips around the yard and through the woods. There's a lot more information about Zipper on my website — he even has his own blog, with lots of pictures! And of course I am planning to write a book about him.

Welcome, Zipper!

Yours from the Puppy Place,
Ellen Miles

DON'T MISS THE
NEXT PUPPY PLACE
ADVENTURE!

Here's a peek at GIZMO!

Dr. Gibson was just as nice as Dr. Garcia, but Buddy did not love going to the vet. "Most of the puppies I've known hate getting shots, too," Charles said to his mother. "Even though Dr. Gibson gives them dog cookies the whole time they're in her exam room." He wondered about that. Maybe Dr. Garcia should hand out people cookies. Would munching on a chocolate-chip cookie make him feel any better about getting shots?

The outside door banged open, and Charles heard kids laughing and shouting. Two little toddlers, about the Bean's age, ran into the waiting room. They looked exactly alike, with brown curls and big brown eyes. They pushed and shoved each other, heading straight for the fish tank. "Don't touch it!" called a voice. A woman with a very, very big belly lumbered after them, sighing as she watched them put their hands — and noses — up against the tank. "Sam, Marco, what did I just tell you?"

At the desk, Martha just shrugged. "It's okay, Mrs. West," she said. "Kids do that all the time."

The woman sighed again and reached for a chair. Holding her belly with one hand, she sank into it. "Come on, boys," she said, patting the seat next to her. "Sit here with me."

"Twins?" Charles's mom asked, smiling.

The woman nodded. She pointed to her stomach. "And triplets on the way — any day now!"

Mom gasped. "You're kidding."

"It's no joke." The woman sighed again. She smiled. "I'll love all five of them, I know I will. But I'll admit it's not what I expected." She sat up straighter and looked around. "Sam? Marco? Where did they get to?"

Charles heard an explosion of giggles from behind the magazine rack.

The woman shook her head. "It's nonstop," she said. "They are always up to something. If they're not climbing on the furniture, they're mushing PLAY-DOH into the rug or stuffing toilet paper into the heating vents. My husband says it's like we already have five kids."

Charles was enjoying this conversation, if only because it took his mind off the shots. "Can you tell them apart?" he asked. From what he had seen, the two boys looked exactly alike.

"Oh, sure," said Mrs. West. "Marco has a dimple in his right cheek, and Sam has a little scar over his eyebrow from the time he ran into an open drawer in the kitchen. And right now, he's got a very runny nose, as well. I think he caught the cold that Marco had last week. That's why we're here."

"Dr. Garcia is ready for you, Charles," said Martha.

Charles frowned. He did not feel ready for Dr. Garcia. He looked at his mom. "Maybe we should let the twins go first," he said.

"That's a nice thought, Charles," said his mother.

"Oh, that would be such a huge help," said the woman. "We have a long list of errands after this, and I don't know how I'm going to get everything done. Boys!"

There was a rustling sound from behind the sofa, and two heads popped up. "Let's get our medicine from Dr. Garcia," she said. "Then we can go let Gizmo out of the car."

"Bad Gizmo!" said Marco.

"Naughty Gizmo," said Sam.

"Who's Gizmo?" asked Charles.

Mrs. West let out one last long sigh as she struggled to her feet. "Believe it or not, on top of everything else, we also have a puppy."

ABOUT THE AUTHOR

Ellen Miles loves dogs, which is why she has a great time writing the Puppy Place books. And guess what? She loves cats, too! (In fact, her very first pet was a beautiful tortoiseshell cat named Jenny.) That's why she came up with the Kitty Corner series. Ellen lives in Vermont and loves to be outdoors every day, walking, biking, skiing, or swimming, depending on the season. She also loves to read, cook, explore her beautiful state, play with dogs, and hang out with friends and family.

Visit Ellen at www.ellenmiles.net.